Amira's FAMILY

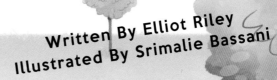

Written By Elliot Riley
Illustrated By Srimalie Bassani

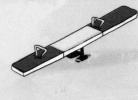

Rourke
Educational Media
rourkeeducationalmedia.com

Before & After Reading Activities

Teaching Focus:

Concepts of Print: Have students find capital letters and punctuation in a sentence. Ask students to explain the purpose for using them in a sentence.

Before Reading:

Building Academic Vocabulary and Background Knowledge

Before reading a book, it is important to set the stage for your child or student by using pre-reading strategies. This will help them develop their vocabulary, increase their reading comprehension, and make connections across the curriculum.

1. Read the title and look at the cover. *Let's make predictions about what this book will be about.*
2. Take a picture walk by talking about the pictures/photographs in the book. Implant the vocabulary as you take the picture walk. Be sure to talk about the text features such as headings, the Table of Contents, glossary, bolded words, captions, charts/diagrams, or Index.
3. Have students read the first page of text with you then have students read the remaining text.
4. Strategy Talk – use to assist students while reading.
   - Get your mouth ready
   - Look at the picture
   - Think…does it make sense
   - Think…does it look right
   - Think…does it sound right
   - Chunk it – by looking for a part you know
5. Read it again.

Content Area Vocabulary
Use glossary words in a sentence.

cashier
country
market
welcome

After Reading:

Comprehension and Extension Activity

After reading the book, work on the following questions with your child or students in order to check their level of reading comprehension and content mastery.

1. *How do Amira's classmates make her feel welcome?* *(Summarize)*
2. *Why did Amira's family move?* *(Asking Questions)*
3. *How is Amira's family like yours? How is it different?* *(Text to self connection)*
4. *What is Amira's favorite activity at school?* *(Asking Questions)*

Extension Activity

Draw a flag for your family! Think about what is important to the people in your family. What do you enjoy? What makes your family special? Create a design that shows these things on your flag. Glue the flag to an empty paper towel roll and wave it proudly!

Table of Contents

Meet Amira

This is Amira.

These are Amira's parents.

Amira's family just
moved to a new **country**.

They left their country when a war started there.

Amira was sad to leave her country.

She was scared to move to a strange new place.

9

New School

Amira's classmates make her feel **welcome.**

They teach her their language. She teaches them her language, too!

Recess is Amira's favorite part of the day.

She likes to swing
and slide.

After school, Amira and her parents go to the **market**.

She sees her new country's flags for sale.

Amira counts her money.

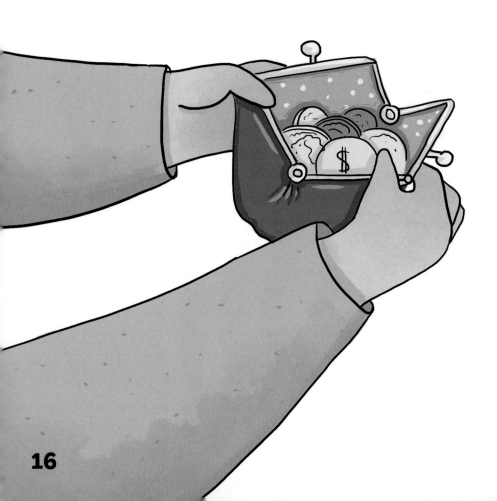

"I would like to buy one flag," she tells the **cashier**.

Welcome Home

Amira puts the flag outside her new house.

"Perfect!" her parents say.

Amira smiles. She is happy they are together and safe.

Amira loves her family.

Amira's family loves her.

Picture Glossary

 **cashier** (ka-SHEER): A person who takes in money at a store.

 **country** (KUHN-tree): A place with its own territory and government.

 **market** (MAHR-kit): A place where people buy and sell food and other items.

 **welcome** (WEL-kuhm): When you welcome someone, you greet them in a nice, friendly way.

Family Fun

Who are the people in your family?

Draw each person and write their name below their picture.

How is your family portrait like Amira's? How is it different?

About the Author

Elliot Riley is an author with a big family of her own in Tampa, Florida. She loves when everyone gets together to eat, laugh, and play games. Especially the eating part!

Meet The Author!
www.meetREMauthors.com

Library of Congress PCN Data

Amira's Family/ Elliot Riley
(All Kinds of Families)
ISBN 978-1-68342-318-8 (hard cover)
ISBN 978-1-68342-414-7 (soft cover)
ISBN 978-1-68342-484-0 (e-Book)
Library of Congress Control Number: 2017931167

Rourke Educational Media
Printed in the United States of America,
North Mankato, Minnesota

www.rourkeeducationalmedia.com

Author Illustration: ©Robert Wicher
Edited by: Keli Sipperley
Cover design and interior design by: Kathy Walsh